D1624514

THE ANGEL
WHO FORGOT

THE ANGEL
WHO FORGOT

By Elisa Bartone
Illustrated by Paul Cline

GREEN TIGER PRESS
Published by Simon & Schuster
New York London Toronto Sydney Tokyo Singapore

GREEN TIGER PRESS
Simon & Schuster Building
Rockefeller Center
1230 Avenue of the Americas
New York, New York 10020

GREEN TIGER PRESS is an imprint of Simon & Schuster.
Manufactured in the United States of America.

10 9 8 7 6 5 4 3 2 1

Library of Congress Cataloging-in-Publication Data
Bartone, Elisa. The angel who forgot / by Elisa Bartone.   p.   cm.
Originally published: La Jolla, Calif. : Green Tiger Press, © 1986.
Summary: The angel who is supposed to cure Miguel has thrown away
his memories and forgotten that he is an angel.   [1. Angels—Fiction.]
I. Title.   PZ7.B28563An   1992   [E]—dc20   91-34233   CIP
ISBN: 0-671-76037-8

To my father with love

EB

For John Kenneth Elliker

PC

Isabella the Beautiful gazed at the rooftop.

She said to the angel who was sitting there, "Come down!"

She wanted to bring him inside to the boy, Miguel. Isabella knew he was the angel who had come to cure him.

But when she called him "angel,"
he protested.

"I am not an angel," said the angel then,
because he had forgotten.

"Don't you know how lovely you are?"
said Isabella the Beautiful.

"No," said the angel, because he had
forgotten.

That night there was thunder and lightning and much rain. The angel sat through it, shivering and shuddering, but never remembering that he was an angel, or that angels can fly.

He was held there by Miguel's wish.

"It was Miguel who dreamed of you, and wished you here to cure him," said Isabella the Beautiful.

"I can't make him better," said the angel, because he had forgotten.

Isabella the Beautiful did not lose hope.

The seasons passed, and she cared for Miguel, and for the angel whom Miguel had wished in his dreams to come cure him.

In the autumn, she covered the roof with blackberry branches and goldenrod, and brought him a wren for company.

In the winter, she covered the roof with snowdrops and holly, and brought him a robin to play with.

In the spring, she covered the roof with wild strawberry and pear blossoms, and brought him a blackbird to sing to him.

In the summer, she covered the roof with
Queen of the Meadow and poppies, and
brought him a dragonfly to pass the
time with.

It was the dragonfly that told Isabella the Beautiful the story of the angel.

"He would *like* to cure Miguel, but he threw away his memories when his heart got broken, and he has forgotten that he is an angel.

"His pony got lost in the forest.

He searched for him night and day.

He could not bear to remember, so he tied his memories to an emerald stone with a piece of string and in a fit of tears threw them into the bottom of Crystal Lake.

"Then," said the dragonfly, "the angel flew to the rooftop where Miguel called him in his dreams, but he could not remember why he was there."

"Take me to Crystal Lake," said Isabella the Beautiful.

She swam to the bottom and . . .

pulled up the emerald stone, which was tied to the angel's memories with a piece of string.

The pony wandered to the lake to the spot where Isabella stood, with the angel's memories in her arms.

The angel took back his memories and rejoiced at the sight of his pony. Finally, he remembered that he was an angel . . .

and . . .

cured Miguel.

Isabella the Beautiful told the angel to hold tight to his memories, because the help of the dragonfly was a miracle of God.

"I am very grateful that you did not lose hope, Isabella the Beautiful," said the angel.

Illustrations are rendered in watercolor.
Text is set in 12 pt. Palatino.